I0591763

Acting Edition

White Pearl

by Anchuli Felicia King

ISBN 978-0-573-71016-2

www.concordtheatricals.com

www.concordtheatricals.co.uk

FOR PRODUCTION INQUIRIES

UNITED STATES AND CANADA
info@concordtheatricals.com
1-866-979-0447

UNITED KINGDOM AND EUROPE
licensing@concordtheatricals.co.uk
020-7054-7298

Each title is subject to availability from Concord Theatricals Corp., depending upon country of performance. Please be aware that *WHITE PEARL* may not be licensed by Concord Theatricals Corp. in your territory. Professional and amateur producers should contact the nearest Concord Theatricals Corp. office or licensing partner to verify availability.

No one shall share this title(s), or any part of this title(s), through any social media or file hosting websites.

For all inquiries regarding motion picture, television, online/digital and other media rights, please contact Concord Theatricals Corp.

MUSIC AND THIRD-PARTY MATERIALS USE NOTE

Licensees are solely responsible for obtaining formal written permission from copyright owners to use copyrighted music and/or other copyrighted third-party materials (e.g., artworks, logos) in the performance of this play and are strongly cautioned to do so. If no such permission is obtained by the licensee, then the licensee must use only original music and materials that the licensee owns and controls. Licensees are solely responsible and liable for clearances of all third-party copyrighted materials, including without limitation music, and shall indemnify the copyright owners of the play(s) and their licensing agent, Concord Theatricals Corp., against any costs, expenses, losses and liabilities arising from the use of such copyrighted third-party materials by licensees. For music, please contact the appropriate music licensing authority in your territory for the rights to any incidental music.

IMPORTANT BILLING AND CREDIT REQUIREMENTS

If you have obtained performance rights to this title, please refer to your licensing agreement for important billing and credit requirements.

AUTHOR'S NOTE

Casting this play is really fucking hard. If you want to put on this play, make sure you have the resources to cast it properly.

Generally speaking, we've found that you can be more flexible with the ethnicity of actors playing the 'Westernized' Asians in the team: Priya, Built, to a certain extent Sunny. And of course Marcel. But the actors *must* have some ethnic or cultural resonance with their character. Have an open dialogue with the actors you're auditioning, reach out to your local Asian theater community, be culturally cognizant, and just generally don't be a dick about it.

With the 'homeland' Asians (Ruki, Soo-Jin and Xiao), it is absolutely imperative that the actors be non-native English speakers from the specific cultural background of their characters. Trust me. I've seen the alternative. It doesn't work.

I don't mind if you move around some of the phraseology but generally speaking, stick to the text. The highly specific language in this play is the result of extensive development, as well as my life experience. There is no one way of speaking Singlish, or Californian English, just as there's no one way to define 'dudebro-speak'. Collaborate with the actors to determine their character's idiosyncratic mode of speaking and their level of English fluency, and be open to adjusting this as your process evolves.

I also strongly recommend you celebrate cultural difference – not just in casting, but in the rehearsal process. A *White Pearl* cast will be a global village, and you'll have a better time if you surround them with creatives and crew members who reflect that cultural multiplicity. I've had the privilege of working with extraordinary women of color throughout the development of this play, and their contributions have enormously informed this playtext.

The final note is about tone. As outlandish as they sometimes are, I don't think any of these characters are parodies. The people in *White Pearl* have absolute conviction about their actions and beliefs. Therefore while the play is certainly a black comedy, bordering on satire, the performances should be grounded, specific and multidimensional. That way it's more horrifying. And funnier.

'/' denotes overlapping dialogue

<u>Underline denotes a projected title card</u>

Bold denotes a YouTube comment.* These can be audio cues or projected. I strongly recommend projected.

The Writer and the Royal Court Theatre wish to make clear that the eponymous product WHITE PEARL and the company CLEAR DAY™ are entirely fictional and any resemblance to existing products or companies is coincidental.

---

* As of this draft, all the comments are real (a few have been slightly edited for length and/or narrative consistency). I haven't changed any of the usernames.

ACKNOWLEDGEMENTS

Thanks to the numerous theaters and institutions that have aided me in the development of this play – Smash the Box Collective, Columbia University, Roundabout Theatre Company, Yellow Earth Theatre, Playwriting Australia and the National Play Festival. At the time of publication, there have been three productions of this play in three different countries; our world premiere at the Royal Court in London, then a national tour of Australia produced by Sydney Theatre Company/National Theatre of Paramatta, and finally the play's American Premiere at Studio Theatre in Washington DC. I'm enormously thankful to all of these companies, not just for taking a chance on this play but for giving me the resources and support to properly stage it.

I am beyond indebted to the huge global family of actors, directors, and creatives who have lent their talent to this play, in particular my collaborator and friend Nana Dakin. When I asked Nana to direct the first ever reading of *White Pearl* in grad school (for no class credit, I should add), I don't think either of us could have ever imagined that we'd be staging it three years later downstairs at the Royal Court. I'm so thrilled and grateful that we've been on this journey together, and cannot thank her enough for her contributions to this play. I also owe an enormous debt to my D.C. director Desdemona Chiang and to Priscilla Jackman, the fearless director of our Australian production, who shepherded an epic, rotating ensemble of actors through a global pandemic as the play toured the country in 2021-2.

Thanks for the ongoing support of my friends and family, my Australian agent Jean Mostyn, my US agents Kevin Lin and Jiah Shin at CAA, and especially m'coll, sister and co-conspirator A.N. King. I dedicate this play to all the gloriously idiosyncratic and ferocious Asian women in my life.

CHARACTERS

PRIYA SINGH – Female. Indian-Singaporean. Mumbai accent, rounded out by years of British education.

SUNNY LEE – Female. Chinese-Singaporean. American dudebro-speak, becomes more Singlish/Hokkien depending on her audience.

RUKI MINAMI – Female. Japanese. Noticeable Japanese accent. Crisp English.

BUILT SUTTIKUL – Female. Thai-American. Californian. Verging on valley-girl.

SOO-JIN PARK – Female. South Korean. Strong Korean accent but excellent English.

XIAO CHEN – Female. Chinese. The weakest English speaker.

MARCEL BENOIT – Male. Strong French accent with fluent-ish English.

All characters are in their mid-twenties / early thirties.

TIME

Present Day.

SETTING

Clearday™ Headquarters, Singapore.

ACT ONE

Scene One: <u>19,643</u>

(A bathroom stall. Dim light.)

(A phone has been discarded next to the toilet.)

(It buzzes mournfully.)

ADELE717 Wtfffffff !!!!!!??????!!!!!!!!!

ZHN0K THIS IS FUCKING FUNNY

(We see **XIAO.***)*

(She is curled up on the floor. Foetal.)

JAY PLAYS GAMES Chinese people eat dogs so I'm not suprise

(She is shaking.)

ÉMILIE 94300 je.suis choquer

CHIANG SHANG 不是什么好人!

AZNYUNGTAH Lmao wow...

ACELAINE23 I'm too shocked to even get mad.

LIN LIN The Great Wall of China just got 10 feet higher

(She sobs.)

Scene Two: <u>20,478</u>

(Conference room. Frosted glass door.)

(A banner reading 'Clear and Bright!'.)

*(**PRIYA** scours the news.)*

*(**SUNNY** holds an unhealthily large ice coffee.)*

PRIYA. What we at?

SUNNY. Twenty K.

PRIYA. So we start, yeah, drafting a statement. As in, draft a statement. As in, draft a statement now. As /in now.

SUNNY. Yeesh, would /you –

PRIYA. Before –

SUNNY. Chill lah.

PRIYA. This is a *catastrophe.* This is a *catastrophe. Chilling* is off the bloody agenda.

SUNNY. Yo – is not.

PRIYA. It's not...?

SUNNY. Catastrophe.

PRIYA. How'd you figure that?

SUNNY. Brand's not even mentioned. And it's like some French account. Who gives a shit about the French?

PRIYA. For *now*, the /brand's not –

SUNNY. Yo, but for real, how somebody *French* get it?

PRIYA. I don't *know.* I don't /*know.*

SUNNY. It's just – you don't think of French people online, eh? You think of them, like –

PRIYA. It shouldn't have *aired.*

SUNNY. Smoking in turtlenecks. Eating baguettes and shit.

PRIYA. I don't know what's *happening.*

SUNNY. It the Chinese one?

PRIYA. Yes.

SUNNY. So call her.

PRIYA. She's *here.*

SUNNY. Huh? She not in Shanghai?

PRIYA. Evidently not.

SUNNY. She in the office?

PRIYA. She went to the *loo.*

SUNNY. Um. Okay?

PRIYA. To the *loo. The loo.*

SUNNY. ...Bro, why you say loo like that?

PRIYA. Half an hour ago.

SUNNY. Ah.

PRIYA. I may have used... extreme language.

SUNNY. Aw. Come on, man.

PRIYA. I wasn't *heartless*, because, yes, she's *delicate.* But this is a professional – it's not an excuse for – I mean, did you *watch* it?

SUNNY. Well, you email at three o' buttcrack dawn so I was barely awake, /but –

PRIYA. And /what –

SUNNY. – seeing as you obviously got no respect for a bro's *kopi** or beauty sleep –

PRIYA. Sunny!

---

* Coffee with condensed milk.

SUNNY. I mean, yeah, man, like you say. It's last like fifteen secs that are the problem.

PRIYA. Did I miss something? Because I thought I made myself abundantly clear.

SUNNY. You did, man, you totally did.

PRIYA. I thought we were all on the same page.

SUNNY. Yeah, no, I know, it's whack that /she could –

PRIYA. Right?

SUNNY. For real.

PRIYA. If something was lost in – because I know her English isn't – not to mention she bursts into tears every time – I mean that's another matter – but but but if this was just blatant disregard –

(**RUKI** *enters, phone in hand.*)

RUKI. There is a reporter calling me?

PRIYA. Shit. Shit. /Shit.

SUNNY. Steady lah.

RUKI. What do I – I have never talked to a /reporter –

SUNNY. Which website?

RUKI. It is not a website – he is from *Japan Today*?

PRIYA. The Japanese have it?

SUNNY. Ruki, how far ahead is Japan?

RUKI. Huh?

PRIYA. The Japanese have it?

SUNNY. Hours, how many hours ahead is Japan?

RUKI. Tokyo is – uh, I think only one hour ahead of us.

PRIYA. The *Japanese* /have it?

SUNNY. Shut up a fuckin' sec, bro – that an English paper? *Japan Today* in English?

RUKI. English? I – I am not sure.

SUNNY. Okay – listen carefully ah? You say 'No comment at this time. We will issue a statement shortly.' Then you hang up and you google *Japan Today.* We don't let this be reported in English. You dig?

RUKI. 'We have no comment at this time. We issue –'

PRIYA. *Will* issue.

RUKI. 'We will issue a statement shortly.' I will tell him.

(**RUKI** *hovers uncertainly.*)

SUNNY. ...Ruki?

RUKI. Yes?

SUNNY. ...

RUKI. ...

SUNNY. ...Now.

RUKI. Oh. Sorry. *(On the phone)* Moshi moshi? Omatase Itashimashita*.

(**RUKI** *exits.*)

(**PRIYA** *grabs* **SUNNY**'s *coffee and takes a sizable gulp.*)

(**SUNNY** *is visibly displeased.*)

PRIYA. Twenty-two – shit, twenty-three thousand.

SUNNY. Okay. We draft a statement *now.*

PRIYA. That's what I bloody /said.

SUNNY. *(grabbing her briefcase)* Imma grab my Mac.

PRIYA. Oh, this is bad. This is so /bad.

---

* Japanese, formal: 'Hello? Thank you for holding.'

SUNNY. Priya. Chill the eff down. *(the coffee)* Drink. US is hours behind. We got time lah.

PRIYA. So we –

SUNNY. Sûnhai kòngzhi*. Find this French ass-clown, get the video taken down. Say big sorry. It's gone before American peeps even wake up. Easy.

PRIYA. The board will want blood for this.

SUNNY. Oh, rest assured, my bro, they gonna KPKB**.

PRIYA. Already think we're bloody inept.

SUNNY. Not us /specifically. If you see what I'm saying.

PRIYA. What? No? What are you saying?

SUNNY. *(indicating the two of them)* Not *us*.

PRIYA. Oh. You're saying like –

SUNNY. Like maybe. I'm saying we got /options.

PRIYA. Hold on hold on. Fuck.

SUNNY. What?

PRIYA. It's on Facebook.

SUNNY. What? /Where?

PRIYA. Look.

SUNNY. Shit. Shit. Okay, uh – report it.

PRIYA. Report –

SUNNY. Click the – there.

PRIYA. What?

SUNNY. The – there – /*ai-ya****.

PRIYA. Where's the – ?

---

* Mandarin: 'damage control'.
** Singlish slang: 'lose their shit'.
*** Cantonese: expression of disappointment, annoyance.

SUNNY. Just – move. Let /me – dude –

PRIYA. What are we reporting?

SUNNY. Duh. Copyright infringement.

PRIYA. Oh. Smart.

SUNNY. Yes, yes, I am.

PRIYA. Wait, so what are we talking here? Are we talking – like, a sacrificial lamb?

SUNNY. Woah, okay bro, don't /be all weird about it.

PRIYA. I'm totally not.

SUNNY. You totally are.

PRIYA. It's not scapegoating if she's, you know. At fault. Which –

SUNNY. Maybe.

PRIYA. We have to – right. Due /diligence.

SUNNY. But we're not talking 'bout that now.

PRIYA. No.

SUNNY. This /first.

PRIYA. But I mean – we're not talking about that? Because somebody's getting fired /for this.

SUNNY. Bro. Not now lah. Now we hustle.

PRIYA. Hustle. Yes.

(Beat.)

SUNNY. Pri.

PRIYA. Mm?

SUNNY. You steal my coffee, you better fuckin' drink it.

Scene Three: <u>48,016</u>

(The bathroom stall.)

*(**SOO-JIN** kneels beside **XIAO** She's still crying.)*

SOO-JIN. But the family friend – the army one – what did he say?

XIAO. He says it is difficult to know. You know, there is some evidence, but they may... they may *make* extra evidence. They are make an example of him.

SOO-JIN. I see.

XIAO. My father is a good man.

SOO-JIN. Of course.

XIAO. Everybody do this in China. It is how you do business. You know? He was just giving gifts. You can not do business without gifts. But now – the Politburo, they are just making show. He is big fish so they make an example. It is not even real clean up. It just for theatre and I am angry at me.

SOO-JIN. It's not your fault.

XIAO. I should be there and help.

SOO-JIN. There is nothing for you to do. Here or there. You stay in China and you will be at risk for your visa for nothing. Your father does not want that.

XIAO. Maybe I testify.

SOO-JIN. This does nothing if the trial is not real. Xiao. Please. There is nothing to do on the toilet floor. Please get up. We have to work.

XIAO. I don't care about this stupid video. This stupid job problem. How can I – when my mother – my *father* –

SOO-JIN. I know.

XIAO. How can I go – and say 'oh yes' and talk about YouTube videos with *them* – when I am –

SOO-JIN. Xiao. Xiao. Okay – once, my supervisor at university – I am trying to do a complicated – to make a chemical. I am running test. And I have just broken up with my stupid ex-boyfriend, you remember I tell you about the stupid one?

XIAO. *(laughing a little in spite of herself)* Yes.

SOO-JIN. So I am synthesizing this chemical. But I am crying, ugly crying, like you now. And eventually I get up, tears are all over my face, and I am saying to my professor: 'I can not do this. I don't feel like it. I am leaving.' You know what he says to me?

XIAO. Mm?

SOO-JIN. 'Soo-Jin, the definition of professional is doing it when you do not feel like it.' We must work. But not this second. We go get KFC first.

XIAO. For breakfast?

SOO-JIN. Eh. Brunch. Why, you don't want KFC?

XIAO. You know I always want KFC.

SOO-JIN. Good. Wash your face.

Scene Four: <u>67,380</u>

(The conference room.)

(**RUKI**, **SUNNY** *and* **PRIYA** *with their laptops.)*

(Lots of KFC.)

SUNNY How's – Priya?

PRIYA Yeah, sorry. Go.

SUNNY Okay. How's this: 'We at Clearday™ would like to extend a profound /apology – '

PRIYA Profound?

SUNNY What?

PRIYA Isn't it, generally, sincere? Our sincere apologies?

SUNNY Our heartfelt apologies?

PRIYA Mm. Sincere. Heartfelt is a bit naff.

SUNNY You're a bit /naff.

RUKI I found something.

PRIYA Where?

SUNNY *Japan Today*?

RUKI *The Times.*

PRIYA *The Times? The /TIMES?*

SUNNY She means the Japanese *Times*.

RUKI Yes – /sorry, I –

PRIYA For the love of – you trying to give me a stroke?

RUKI I'm /sorry!

SUNNY It's cool, Ruki, it's cool. They list a source?

RUKI I am not sure. Let me – I do not see – no, it just says the YouTube account.

PRIYA 'lafemmeirigary636.' Who the fuck are you?

SUNNY It's gotta be French, yah? Cuz I can't find this username like anywhere else.

PRIYA What about that last bit, I-ri Ga-ry? What is that?

SUNNY I dunno, bro. Sounds Japanese.

RUKI It is definitely not Japanese.

SUNNY I didn't say it *was* Japanese. I said it *sounds* Japanese.

RUKI I am Japanese. It does not sound Japanese.

PRIYA Have we investigated – I don't know, French TV people? Is there like a database of French TV people working in China?

SUNNY Bro. That's so not a thing.

PRIYA I don't know!

SUNNY Weren't you supposed to be getting DBB?

PRIYA They're calling me back. They need a fucking translator.

SUNNY Dude, what?

PRIYA Yep.

SUNNY They're an international ad agency.

PRIYA I know.

SUNNY They're an international ad agency and no one in the office speak fuckin' English?

PRIYA Think you can hash it out in Mandarin?

SUNNY *Hell* no.

PRIYA Fuck.

SUNNY Sure wish we had a Chinese in the office. Like, gee, dunno lah, maybe even like the head of the Chinese branch ah? Maybe the person who hire the fuckin' agency in the first place. Like that sort of a person.

PRIYA Soo-Jin's on it.

SUNNY Eh?

PRIYA She just texted. She's with her.

SUNNY In the *toilet*?

PRIYA Apparently.

SUNNY What, they taking a twin shit?

PRIYA She's *consoling* her.

SUNNY Well, whenever Miss China decides to quit pang seh* *(pointed look at* **PRIYA***)* we – you know. We grill her la.

PRIYA I know. /I know.

RUKI *(has never heard this expression, takes it literally, is justifiably confused)* ...Grill... her? With a... grill?

SUNNY Nah, man. Wok-fry. Sssss.

*(**BUILT** enters, all sunglasses and tote.)*

(She is chuckling at something on her phone.)

BUILT Morning, ladies.

PRIYA Nice of you to join us.

SUNNY It's midday, asshole.

BUILT Ahem. *(reading off her phone)* 'Racist ad goes viral.'

PRIYA Fuck.

BUILT 'A Pan-Asian cosmetics firm –'

SUNNY See? Brand /not mention, ah?

BUILT '– has been attacked on social media today for a series of offensive ads –'

---

* Singaporean slang: 'Abandoning us'.

PRIYA This is bad. This is so bad.

BUILT I'll just like skip some of the fat – oookay, soooo – the synopsis. Which, by the way, is like *super* dramatic.

SUNNY I hate you so hard.

BUILT 'The ad campaign tells the story of a young dark-skinned Chinese woman who is left by her boyfriend for an evil lighter-skinned woman. Distraught, our heroine takes a trip to her local supermarket to buy ice cream, only to be stopped by an angelic store clerk with a white halo, who recommends that she try the Clearday™ –'

SUNNY /Wah lau eh*. Why they say the fuckin' brand.

BUILT /' – *White Pearl* cream. In the second segment, the young woman uses the cream, becomes whiter, wins her boyfriend back and becomes a famous actress.' So good so far. Buuuut... oh, what's this? 'In the final segment –'

RUKI This is...not /the *Times* article.

BUILT ' – as the happily reunited couple stroll along the beach, the evil lighter-skinned woman watches them at a distance. She produces –' *(Her phone starts to ring.)* ew, shut up – sorry – *(scrolling back)* blah blah blah, okay – 'she produces a tub of *White Pearl*, and *desperately* lathers it on. But instead of becoming whiter, her skin turns black and her hair poofs into an afro. As hip-hop blares, the woman catches sight of herself in a shop window and screams in horror. In Mandarin, a voice announces '*White Pearl*. Warning: only works on inner beauty.' The woman then explodes in a cloud of black smoke.'

PRIYA *(despairing)* Did they have to put in everything?

RUKI Where is this article?

BUILT Hold on to your cunts... *Buzzfeed*.

PRIYA No.

---

* Hokkien phrase: 'My father eh' – conveying shock, disappointment.

SUNNY Motherfucker.

RUKI Sorry, what is Buzz Feed?

PRIYA It's like news for people who don't read the news – *(to* **BUILT***)* are you *laughing*?

BUILT Honey, this is the end of our careers. I'm riding the tide.

SUNNY Bro ya'fucked too.

BUILT Sweetie, I've got a rich daddy. I'll go like chill all high-so* in Bangkok. It's the rest of y'all that are *(sing-song)* screwwwed.

PRIYA No one here – no one's career is – just to be clear – just to be perfectly clear – this is the first point in the press release – Clearday™ did not okay this.

BUILT Say what now?

PRIYA We didn't.

BUILT Um, so we're like lying?

PRIYA We didn't okay it!

BUILT We like totally did.

PRIYA No. NO! They pitched the smoke but there was no discussion of an *afro*. Of *hip-hop*. Of *blackface*. And anyway, I thought it was clear – it was made *abundantly* clear that we wanted the third part *excised*.

BUILT Hm. That's like not at all what I remember.

PRIYA Oh?

BUILT No, I like pretty clearly remember that you left it to her quote */discretion* unquote.

SUNNY My God – look, party line – 'We at Clearday™ would like to apologize sincerely for any offense caused by the White Pearl advertisement.'

---

* High-society.

RUKI Excuse me –

SUNNY 'Clearday™ was unaware that the DBB Advertising Agency, which was hired by the Chinese branch of our organization –'

RUKI Excuse me –

SUNNY ' – expanded on the outline that they originally /showed us.'

RUKI I'm sorry –

PRIYA What, Ruki, WHAT.

RUKI Just... should we only be saying that the ad is racist?

PRIYA Uh. Yes?

RUKI I mean, of course, the ad is racist. But maybe we should also be saying that this is not the... the *message* of the ad? The evil woman – the point is that *Pearl* reveals her black soul. It is a metaphor about... about, um, inner beauty? Whitening cream is about showing an inner beauty? And that is a positive statement for women. For global women.

BUILT *(slow clap)* Give this bitch an Oscar.

PRIYA It's on *Buzzfeed*.

SUNNY I mean, we *could* –

PRIYA It's on *BUZZFEED*. It's on *BUZZFEED*. We're not / *defending* it.

SUNNY Woah woah woah, dudes, we jumped big time.

BUILT How much?

SUNNY Like three hundred K lah.

PRIYA What?

SUNNY Is that – yeah, no. Four hundred thousand views, yo.

BUILT *Buzzfeed*. Who knew.

PRIYA For the love of – somebody please get me this French YouTube *reprobate*.

RUKI Oh, I think I have something to do with that.

PRIYA Well, for fuck's – you've got vocal chords, Ruki! Use them!

RUKI Okay, okay, so. It is a very new account. I think this profile was made just for this video. So it is not part of a channel of racist ads. But there is no email for the owner of the channel.

PRIYA So... did you actually find anything?

RUKI ...No.

PRIYA Well. That's bloody useless, isn't /it.

RUKI Oh! Yes – I did – it is not Iri Gary.

PRIYA Iri...?

RUKI The username. I think it is La Femme Irigary. Irigary one word.

SUNNY So it *is* Japanese.

RUKI *No*. I think maybe it is a typo. And that is why we could not find anything. Iri *G-A-R-A-Y* is the name of a famous French feminist.

SUNNY Abuden*.

PRIYA Wait, you're telling me that this bitch is... what, a French feminazi? A *guerilla French feminazi*?

RUKI Gorilla? You mean like a /monkey?

BUILT Oh yeah like, totally, one of those like super famous Chinese-French feminazis. Who like regularly misspell the names of famous French feminazis. One of those.

SUNNY Wait – so what – a French feminazi is, what, chillin' in Shanghai, watching TV, casually uploads a racist ad?

RUKI Maybe she is actually Chinese and just uses French to be classy. Many people use French to be more classy.

---

* Singlish: 'Obviously' or 'of course' – used sarcastically.

BUILT It doesn't even like make sense. This like totally isn't even a feminist thing. This is like a race thing.

RUKI *(genuine)* Can it not be both things?

PRIYA Ladies! This is – we're getting distracted – no one was watching this on TV. This didn't air in Shanghai. This *can't* have aired. They can't just distribute ads without our consent.

SUNNY Unless they got our go.

BUILT Ooh. You think...?

SUNNY Maybe.

PRIYA No!

BUILT But like... maybe?

PRIYA She wouldn't do that.

SUNNY She wouldn't, ah?

PRIYA No. Oh, God. Maybe. I don't know.

BUILT She has been like a total wildcard lately.

PRIYA Look. For her sake –

  *(**PRIYA**'s phone rings.)*

SUNNY Is it DBB?

PRIYA Finally. *(into phone)* Ni hao – oh, thank Christ.

BUILT *(laughing)* Ask if they recently hired any French feminists!

SUNNY *(to **BUILT**)* You are the literal worst.

PRIYA *(into phone)* I've /been – wait, ask her if it aired.

BUILT You love me.

SUNNY Uh, I love you like I love a rectal exam.

PRIYA Can she put me on to someone who *does* /know?

SUNNY I love you like I love a /shot to the groin.

PRIYA What do you – no, don't /put me on hold!

SUNNY I love you like I love Boko /fuckin' Haram.

PRIYA I'M NOT INTERESTED IN YOUR MEDIOCRITY, WOMAN! GET ME ANSWERS!

Scene Five: <u>467,327</u>

(The lobby of Clearday™ HQ.)

*(**MARCEL** slouches in a couch with his laptop.)*

(He is slurping a colossal bubble tea. Like – colossal.)

(French rap blaring audibly from his headphones.)

(At length, he picks up his phone.)

MARCEL Hello, may I speak to your editor? *(beat)* I would like to be anonymous. *(beat)* It is about the racist Chinese ad that is going viral? I have a source. *(beat)* Could he call me back on this number? *(beat)* Okay, thank you.

(He hangs up. He googles some more. He redials.)

Hello, may I speak to your editor? *(beat)* I would like to be anonymous. *(beat)* It is about the racist Chinese ad that is going viral? *(beat)* Okay, thank you. You call on this number if you change your mind. *(beat)* Okay. *(beat)* You also.

(He hangs up. He unfolds a piece of paper. He peruses it. He redials. He gets to voicemail.)

Answer your phone.

You have seen the video.

I am downstairs.

(He hesitates).

I love you.

(He hangs up.)

Scene Six: <u>654,398</u>

(The full team.)

*(**XIAO** and **SOO-JIN** on one side of the table.)*

*(**PRIYA**, **SUNNY** and **BUILT** on the other.)*

*(**RUKI** hovers uncertainly.)*

XIAO *(looking at her shoes)* I have make some mistakes.

PRIYA Here is a list of things you approved.

XIAO I am admitting /to my mistake.

PRIYA Number one: Afro. Number two: Addition of hip-hop. Number three –

XIAO Please –

PRIYA BLACKFACE.

XIAO Please listen –

PRIYA YOU APPROVED THE USE OF *BLACKFACE*.

XIAO The agency – please listen –

PRIYA DO YOU UNDERSTAND THE *HISTORICAL SIGNIFICANCE OF BLACKFACE.*

XIAO Please, the agency – they tell me we need make it more funny. If we CGI her skin turns dark, it is not funny. It will be same as all other whitening cream ad. They want it to be viral in China. They want it to be sensation.

PRIYA Well, they got their bloody wish!

XIAO You must believe – I did not approve this cut.

PRIYA DBB says otherwise.

XIAO I did not –

PRIYA Then who approved it?

XIAO I don't know! Maybe they lying to save face. You must believe – I wait to come back from Shanghai, so we watch and discuss together. I know maybe you will have some issues. This is a rough cut. It's never on T.V. I do not know how this happen. You must believe me.

PRIYA That's not even – if you think that /absolves you –

*(**BUILT**'s phone buzzes. She takes it off the table.)*

BUILT Sorry.

(Uncomfortable beat.)

SUNNY 'Kay um, I'm sending the release, any edits?

SOO-JIN This is the press release in the dropbox?

SUNNY Yeah?

SOO-JIN Oh, this is not a good idea. I will redraft this.

SUNNY Uh. Your head* you will.

SOO-JIN This apology is short-term thinking. I am trying here to be thinking of the future, of the future of this brand, beyond this immediate second. After this problem is over. Okay?

PRIYA I don't see how –

SOO-JIN Obviously, worstcase scenario there will be some anger, mostly from the American Ethnic Negro Community who do not understand it is a joke. But our consumers are not Negroes/ or even –

PRIYA Oh my God, somebody /please –

BUILT Sweetheart, you don't say negro.

SOO-JIN Mm?

BUILT Negro is like offensive. It's like a slur.

SOO-JIN No.

---

* Singlish: used to disabuse someone of a bad idea or erroneous attempt.

BUILT Yes.

SOO-JIN No. The slur is N – /

PRIYA Don't!

SUNNY Aw /shit.

BUILT Okay, definitely don't say that. We say black now.

SOO-JIN Black?

BUILT Like, black people.

RUKI This is correct, Soo-Jin.

SOO-JIN No, no, in all my English studies at university we are referring to them as Negroes. It is ethnic anthropology. Like pygmies.

BUILT Well, sweetheart, I know jackshit about anthropology, but we say black.

SOO-JIN Okay, black, negro, doesn't matter.

SUNNY Kinda does /matter.

SOO-JIN The point I am making is that our customers are not black whatever Americans or British people. They are Asians. They are Asian women. And so, yes, worstcase scenario for a few days – maybe even weeks – our brand will get anger from the West. Maybe a *tiny* bit of this anger will come from Asia too, but it will mostly be coming from the West. We agree about this?

PRIYA What's your –

SOO-JIN What I am saying is that after this anger is over, then we must going back to our business. We must repair the damage. So what I am saying is we do not want to panic and give in to these few angry reactions. We do not want to send the message to our customers – who will mostly not find this video to be racist but actually very funny – we do not want to send the message that we give in to the crazy Western response. We do not want to be seen as saying yes to American PC Culture. We do not want to be sending the message that yes, so sorry, stupid Asians are so racist.

BUILT Um, like, Asians are super racist.

SOO-JIN You think this only because you are not actually Asian.

BUILT Uh –

SOO-JIN You have been raised and your education is from America. Your view is American. Like Priya's is British. I have a more Asian perspective because I am really an Asian.

BUILT Bitch say what.

PRIYA Leave it, she doesn't know what /she's saying.

SOO-JIN Please do not speak for me. I know exactly what I am saying.

PRIYA Well, look, Soo, we appreciate your input /but –

SOO-JIN No, no – please listen to what I am saying. Where we sell – this is Thailand, China, Philippines – these countries are still one race only. Asians, ordinary Asians, they still think that blacks are dirty, smell bad, are criminals. Many of these people never have seen a black person. So we do not want to be siding with the blacks –

PRIYA But /you –

SOO-JIN – we must be on the side of our customers.

PRIYA We can't just assume – I mean, *you* don't think that. As the self-proclaimed 'authentic' Asian in the room, *you* don't think that black people, that they're, what...foul-smelling criminals.

SOO-JIN ...

PRIYA Soo? You... you don't think that.

SOO-JIN We are selling whiteness here. Black is the opposite of white. We do not side with black. This is my professional opinion.

PRIYA Oh my God.

SOO-JIN This is not about my /personal opinion.

PRIYA You do. You do.

SOO-JIN No.

PRIYA No?

SOO-JIN Of course I understand it is more complicated.

PRIYA That it's more 'complicated'.

SOO-JIN Blacks in Asia are not the same as blacks in America. In America, you have Beyoncé, Oprah, Obama.

BUILT Ooh, I love him.

SOO-JIN In Asia, the blacks are poor, they are immigrant, they are homeless, they commit many crimes. They are a burden.

SUNNY Shit, son. I'm out.

SOO-JIN And anyway it is not blacks so much that smell bad, it is Indians and Middle Easterns.

PRIYA *Excuse* me?

SOO-JIN Oh, you are not Indian-smelling.

SUNNY Hoo. We're going there.

SOO-JIN You wear a lot of deodorant and do not eat spices.

PRIYA Excuse me, who – who are you again? Are you part of the management team? Oh, oh no, that's right, you're the *chemical consultant*. You're the Korean *chemical consultant*. So unless your bloody racist crock has any direct bearing on what we can get away with in terms of dosage – you need to sit back and *shut the fuck up*. You will not be redrafting *shit*. You will sit there and shut up and be *racist* and *Korean*. You will sit and shut up and eat your fucking *bibimbap* and praise your glorious leader.

SOO-JIN That is North Korea! I am from South Korea! It is a completely different country!

(**BUILT**'s *phone buzzes a second time.*)

(*She mouths an apology and picks it up.*)

BUILT Clearday™. Uh-huh. (*stepping outside*) ...Who is this?

(**BUILT** *exits.*)

XIAO (*speaking up after a long silence, on the verge of a full breakdown*) I just...I want to say...that I am very sorry. For any trouble – I am very sorry. /I did not –

PRIYA Jesus.

XIAO – mean – I have let the team down. It is my fault. Please do not fight and insult. Please do not angry with each other. You blame me. It is my – m-my fault.

RUKI It's okay, Xiao.

PRIYA No. No, it's not. Don't let her off because she's *crying*. What, you think you're absolved because you're crying? Is that it? You think you get a pass because you're *sad*?

XIAO I – I – I am sorry –

PRIYA Because you're bloody *sad*?

SUNNY Bro.

PRIYA If I got a pass every time I was sad, I'D BE A FUCKING PASS COLLECTOR!

SUNNY Bro, come on. Ease /up.

PRIYA I'D BE FUCKING DRIPPING IN PASSES!

SUNNY Hey! Bro! Enough.

PRIYA No! This is a *workplace*. We do not excuse people because they're *hysterical*.

XIAO (*blubbering*) I am so – so – sorry.

PRIYA This is pathetic. Just – clean yourself up.

(**XIAO** *exits, weeping.* **SOO-JIN** *moves to follow her.*)

(She stops at the door.)

SOO-JIN Priya.

PRIYA Soo-Jin.

SOO-JIN You're a fascist.

*(**SOO-JIN** slams the door behind her. Hard.)*

PRIYA *(under her breath)* And you're a racist cunt.

(The glass door cracks.)

SUNNY *Ai-ya.*

Scene Seven: <u>977,803</u>

(The lobby of Clearday™ HQ.)

(MARCEL and BUILT across from each other.0

MARCEL *(unfolding a piece of paper)* In preparation, I have written some things I would like to say to you.

BUILT This is happening.

MARCEL 'When you walked away from me –'

BUILT This is actually happening.

MARCEL ' – I felt as though I was a piece of junk –'

BUILT You're in my lobby.

MARCEL '– thrown away and sinking to the bottom of the gutter.'

BUILT My lobby. In Singapore.

MARCEL 'When I was with you, my heart, it was like a child, but today that child is dying of leukemia –'

BUILT Oh my god –

MARCEL '– he is gone bald and starving –'

BUILT Oh my God, stop, Marcel, just – stop. Just stop.

MARCEL I have missed you every single day.

BUILT Nhhhh –

MARCEL I need you to hear –

BUILT Nhhhhh. Nhh.

MARCEL – that I am truly sorry.

BUILT You're... sorry.

MARCEL Yes.

BUILT You're sorry. You're sorry. Like, uh, tell me, Marcel, out of interest, what specifically are you sorry for?

MARCEL For the way we have drifted apart.

BUILT Oh, that's, that's what you're sorry for.

MARCEL Yes.

BUILT That we've *drifted apart.*

MARCEL Of course.

BUILT Not for like, I don't know, random example, like, the time you threw a blender at my *face*? Or like the time you like stalked me to Bangkok when I moved from LA *to get away from you*, and then you like attacked me in the Hilton lobby, and my dad had you arrested and deported?

MARCEL You exaggerate.

BUILT That is a *literal description of what happened.*

MARCEL I will not be sorry for the way I fight for you.

BUILT So you know, how girls have like... crazy ex stories? Like about exes who like barricaded themselves in their rooms or climbed up their fire escape and like skinned their cats and shit? Yeah, so – just to be perfectly clear – you are that person to me. You are like my crazy French ex. I like tell other girls horror stories about you. So – like, you're *that*. We are *that*. We are not some romantically fucked-up across-the-sea lifetime movie bullshit like you think we are. You are a scary person. You are a fucked-up person. And this is like stalking. And this is like blackmail. And like I should totally call the police, but I fucking won't, because like, as you know, I can't really do that, because you like currently have the fate of my entire company in your sick fucking hands. So like ultimately I'm almost fascinated to see where you're going with this, but I really think that you should like know upfront before we get into this conversation that there is not even a single part of me, like literally not even an iota, that would ever, like in a million years, want to get back together with you. Like ever. So – keeping that in mind – like, what are your fucking demands?

MARCEL Get back together with me.

BUILT *(throwing her hands in the air)* ...I can't. I can't.

MARCEL Come home with me.

BUILT Like can you please – like how actually do you see this playing out? Like, tell me, for actual, how do you see this scenario playing out?

MARCEL You want to talk *scenario**?

BUILT Yeah. I want to talk *(mimicking him) scenario.*

MARCEL Okay. Here is *scenario*. I am on a shoot, a lifestyle shoot for a big brand in Shanghai. I collaborate with this very talented, very big videographer, also works in Asia – Italian guy named Marco, very cool guy. And Marco, one day on set, he is telling me this crazy story – he says 'Two weeks ago, I make this super racist commercial for Clearday™.' And I am thinking 'Clearday™. Hm.' Something is catching my interest about this Clearday™, something in the back of my brain, but I cannot quite... situate it. So that night after the shoot, I am going home and googling this Clearday™ and *boom* – wheels are starting to turn in my brain – this is the company of the job that my little Built works. And look too, she has a promotion! Some fancy big Product Manager position now. Here is a photo of her all corporate with her high heels and little skirt and the cream in her hand. Very sexy. So now I am getting creative – you know like how creative am I, baby – and I am calling Marco and saying 'Hey Marco, my man, I am chilling here in my hotel, nothing happening, you want to maybe have a drink – oh and maybe bring your laptop, we drink and watch that super racist ad?' So Marco is coming over and you know these Italians can *drink* so of course I am giving him bottle and bottle and bottle of wine and we are laughing and having a great time, watching this racist ad. So fast forward

---

* In French, 'scenario' has more narrative connotations, it also means story, script, screenplay.

one a.m., Marco is very drunk and sleepy and he is wanting to go but I am saying 'No, no, this area is dangerous, sleep on the couch' until eventually he is agreeing. And when I am sure he is dead to the light, easy as easy, I take his laptop. And within – has it been even, what, forty-eight hours? – *voilá*. One million views.

BUILT And the Eerie–Carry thing?

MARCEL Eh?

BUILT The YouTube account, the like – the feminist name thing, what is that about?

MARCEL Oh, Irigaray? *(chuckling)* That is – that is – how you say – an inside joke. Between you and me.

BUILT ...

MARCEL Because you are saying all the time I hate woman. That I am misogynist. This is the joke.

BUILT ...I don't think you understand what a joke is.

MARCEL Look, I can see what you are thinking – he is crazy. What is he thinking. Mm? Okay. What I'm thinking, is, I am coming here, you are angry and disgusted but also maybe a little impressed and turned on, okay, your ego is flattered, we are back in our little games together. So I take the video down, and you come home with me.

BUILT Yep. You're crazy.

MARCEL In the second scenario, you are calling me crazy. Which you know I do not like to be called. So I call my contact at the *New York Times* and I give interviews on how I liberée and upload the video. My website gets traffic, I get more job, I am famous in many countries – I am a – a – what, a *social justice warrior*, good poster boy, handsome French boy, non? So it's sort of, you know, win-win for me at this point. Of course, I would prefer the first.

BUILT You know what? Whatever. It's had like a million views. Damage done. Like leave it up forever for all I care. Talk to anyone you want. I'm over this. Get out.

MARCEL If that's the way you feel.

BUILT That *is* the way I feel.

MARCEL So how you feel about a jail term?

BUILT ...What?

MARCEL Scandal rarely comes *sans* jail term, ah?

BUILT Are you completely – no one's going to *prosecute* us. What the hell? Like arrest us over a racist Chinese ad?

MARCEL Over the ad? Oh, nobody.

BUILT Marcel, what the eff are you talking about?

MARCEL You think I am coming here with only one card under my sleeve?

BUILT So that's like not even /the expression.

MARCEL I know shit.

BUILT Pssh. You don't know shit.

MARCEL Okay. Sure. I don't know shit.

BUILT Wait, do you know shit?

MARCEL I know some shit.

BUILT What kind of shit?

MARCEL Shit like... *(mimicking her)* 'because the exchange rates are changing all time –'

BUILT Oh my God.

MARCEL '– and I am translating the Thai tax returns –'

BUILT Oh my God.

MARCEL Or maybe Clearday™ changes their policy on embezzlement?

BUILT OhmyGodOhmyGodOhmyGod.

MARCEL And here you talk to me as if I am the psychopath. Mm? We are both psychopaths, baby. It is why we fit together. In this life and every other life, we are one. And you cannot see this, so you leave me. You leave and it breaks me apart into pieces but I try to live. I focus on my work. And my work is good. I am a real artist now. I am a big success. My photos are being across Asia. I get the cover of the Japanese *Vogue*. I do well. And just when I think I am ready to forget, and I almost a person again, then fate which is cruel puts you again in my lap. The universe will not let me forget. So – the expression in English – this is the hand we are dealt. N'est pas? Donc. You make me suffer. Now I make you suffer.

BUILT How much? To make this go away. How much?

MARCEL Ohh, baby, non, non, for the first time in your life, this is not a problem you can buy your way out. You have two option. Option one: you go to jail. Option deux: you come home with me.

(*Beat.*)

BUILT Option 3.

MARCEL There is no –

BUILT I'll blow you.

MARCEL What?

BUILT Take it down. I'll blow you.

MARCEL ...Here?

BUILT No, not here. (*beat*) In the bathroom.

MARCEL Oh. Ohhhh, Built.

BUILT This is like strictly a one-time offer.

MARCEL You are a sick little puppy.

BUILT You have to *disappear*. I like don't wanna hear you, I don't wanna see you, you have to like *vanish*.

MARCEL We fit together, baby.

BUILT Going once.

MARCEL Come home with me.

BUILT Going twice.

MARCEL Please –

BUILT Going three times.

MARCEL Come home.

BUILT Aaand –

MARCEL Okay! Okay.

BUILT Okay?

MARCEL Okay.

BUILT Okay. If the video is down in, like, ten minutes, you meet me in the bathroom.

MARCEL Uh–uh, – first blowjob, then I take it down.

BUILT OhmyGod, Marcel, this is not a fucking hostage negotiation. *(beat)* Fine, whatever.

MARCEL It must be a good one.

BUILT Um. It's me. It'll be good.

MARCEL And long.

BUILT Dude, that's on you.

MARCEL And no teeth.

BUILT Ew. Meet me in the bathroom.

Scene Eight: <u>1.2 Million</u>

(The bathroom stall.)

*(**XIAO**, still weeping.)*

*(**SOO-JIN** kneeling beside her.)*

XIAO I – I am so s–sorry. I am so –

SOO-JIN Stop. Stop. It is them who should be saying sorry.

XIAO No, no. They are right. I am pathetic. I am weak. I am not strong like Priya. I am too weak to say no to DBB. I am too weak to defend my family. I just run away and cry. I am just stupid and weak. Weak weak weak.

SOO-JIN You are not the weak one. Listen to me. Priya has not done what you are doing. None of those American British schoolgirls have done what you are doing. They have never had real hardship. They do not understand suffering. They are just bitches.

XIAO *(stunned)* Soo!

SOO-JIN They are. They are bitches.

XIAO They are not –

SOO-JIN No. They are *bitches*. BITCHES. Say it.

XIAO They are...

SOO-JIN Bitches.

XIAO They are...

SOO-JIN *Bitches*.

XIAO They – they are – *(softly)* bitches.

SOO-JIN One more.

XIAO *(giggles)* Bitches.

SOO-JIN Louder.

XIAO *(a torrent)* BITCHES. BITCHES /BITCHES BITCHES.

SOO-JIN YES! /FUCKING BITCHES!

XIAO F-FUCK BITCHES! FUCKING BITCHES! BITCHES!

(Their shrieks devolve into hysterical laughter.)

(At length, they settle.)

I approved the ad.

SOO-JIN I know.

XIAO I just know they would not like it. I was coming back from Shanghai and I know they not like it. All this time and money and danger I put into making this ad, good ad, funny ad – all the time I am in Shanghai they watch me, put car outside my house, listen in my phone – and all the time there will be no point, will be waste, because these... these... these *bitches* will not like it.

SOO-JIN I like it.

XIAO You do?

SOO-JIN Of course. It's funny.

XIAO It is?

SOO-JIN Very funny.

XIAO You like all of it? The hip-hop?

SOO-JIN When her hair – I laughed so much.

XIAO Really?

SOO-JIN I nearly peed!

XIAO Yes! Why they take it so serious? It is like they cannot understand when joke is joke. It is not some big politics whatever. It is just fun ad. Now the whole world is going crazy.

SOO-JIN Asia will not go crazy. We'll be fine.

XIAO Soo?

SOO-JIN Yes?

XIAO Do you think they will tell board to fire me?

SOO-JIN *(honest)* I – I don't know.

XIAO You know – my work visa –

SOO-JIN ...Oh.

XIAO I cannot go back. Not now. It getting so much worse. I cannot be fired. Please – you must help me.

SOO-JIN I – they do not listen to me. You see /how –

XIAO Please.

SOO-JIN There is /nothing –

XIAO Please, Soo.

SOO-JIN There is nothing I can do.

XIAO I am beg you. I go back and they will watch me. Just because I am my father's daughter, they watch me. They watch me forever. I need visa. Please, Soo.

SOO-JIN I – I do not know what you are asking me to do.

XIAO You know things.

SOO-JIN ...Things?

XIAO You are scientist. You know things. Thing that we are doing here. Thing that could help me.

SOO-JIN I – I don't know what you are talking about.

XIAO You say – if they try to fire me, you will tell things. To the newspaper. Now we are watched. You tell the things you know.

SOO-JIN There is nothing to tell.

XIAO Now you are lying to me.

SOO-JIN No! Xiao, everything we do here – there is some of it that is... grey area, okay? But what you are asking, it would take something *illegal*. There is nothing like that.

XIAO Then... then you lie.

SOO-JIN ...What?

XIAO How will they know? None of us are knowing anything about chemicals. You lie. You say we are doing something not legal somewhere. To make – to make it more whitening!

SOO-JIN Xiao! Are you crazy? I cannot say I have been – then that will be *my* problem, you understand? Then they will fire me!

XIAO Not if you say you will talk to newspaper. We are already sink. They will not want make things worse.

SOO-JIN I cannot do what you are asking me.

XIAO Soo. When I am in Shanghai, a man follow me in black Mercedes. Every minute. I see car outside my window every night. I can not sleep for more than three hours. At the airport, they hold me for four hours. They hold me four hours and they – okay – they take my clothing. I am naked while a fat army woman is poking at – she is poking at my everything. This is not a joke for me. People disappear in China, Soo. I do not want disappear.

SOO-JIN I –

XIAO Help me. I beg you.

SOO-JIN Xiao –

XIAO I beg you.

SOO-JIN I – I will think. Okay? I cannot promise but I will think.

XIAO No. You must promise. You will save my freedom. I beg you. Or we are not friends.

Scene Nine: <u>1.9 Million</u>

(The conference room.)

*(***RUKI*** *is on the other side of the door, feebly fixing the cracked glass with masking tape.)*

*(***SUNNY*** *and* ***PRIYA*** *at the table.)*

PRIYA Well.

SUNNY Yeahhh.

PRIYA So this is a fucking shitshow.

SUNNY You're telling me.

PRIYA The fucking /nerve, I mean –

SUNNY Gabra*, bro.

PRIYA So.

SUNNY Uh-huh.

PRIYA Board meeting tomorrow.

SUNNY Uh-huh.

PRIYA Someone's getting fired.

SUNNY You think.

PRIYA Well. So. Actually.

SUNNY Huh?

PRIYA Maybe not *someone*.

SUNNY Don't follow.

PRIYA Maybe... some *people*.

SUNNY Huh? Oh. *Oh*.

---

* Singlish: 'chaos'.

PRIYA I mean, because – obviously Xiao has to go. Obviously. I mean I feel bad for the girl, I do, but –

SUNNY World˙. You don't feel bad.

PRIYA No. I don't. She's a fucking idiot.

SUNNY Man, is she like – safe? If she's deported?

PRIYA Leave off. China's no more fucked-up than here. If you've got money and connections – which the girl obviously does, I mean look at that nose job – she's fine.

SUNNY Yeah.

PRIYA Exactly.

SUNNY Okay. Cool. So what are we talking here?

PRIYA If we were to – in the course of the meeting, bring up, for example, in addition to the *staggering* Chinese mismanagement of this crisis, if we were to bring up someone else's – let's say – problematic stance.

SUNNY Ah.

PRIYA General… political outlook and so forth.

SUNNY Ah.

PRIYA Not to mention damage of company property.

SUNNY Dude, you are epic level heartless right now. I love it.

PRIYA Hey, hey, no, come on, this isn't *personal*. She's racist. She's a liability. Particularly in the wake of all of this. We can't have someone like that on our team. I mean, a racist Korean after racist ad fallout? Disaster in wait.

SUNNY Bro. You don't have to sell me. Girl a pain in my ass for years, much as yours. Root the weed.

PRIYA Okay. Okay. Big day. Big changeover. Excellent. Really excellent. I'm feeling good about this.

˙ Singlish: 'bullshit'.

SUNNY Now what?

PRIYA Well. Prep for the board. HR. Severance. Call the building manager about the fucking door. Then... you know. Business as usual.

SUNNY 'Til something else gets leaked. Lol.

PRIYA God forbid.

SUNNY And the video? We just leave it?

PRIYA Unless Iri-ma-fucking-Gary emerges. Look, the damage is bloody well done. No sense expending the energy. Look to the future.

SUNNY Right on.

PRIYA Speaking of – what we at?

SUNNY *(checking)* Ha!

PRIYA That bad?

SUNNY Bro, we a gone-case*.

PRIYA Come on then.

SUNNY Three. Point. One. Million.

PRIYA *(laughing)* Jesus. Jesus.

SUNNY This day lah.

PRIYA Break out the whisky?

SUNNY Ger**, get out my brain.

---

* Singlish: 'doomed'.
** Singlish: 'Girl'.

ACT TWO

Scene One: <u>One Year Ago</u>

(The conference room. Cleaner. Cheaper chairs. No banner.)

SUNNY *and* **RUKI** *enter.*

SUNNY How long you been here?

RUKI Here?

SUNNY In Singapore.

RUKI Almost... one year.

SUNNY Oh! Oh sweet, thought you was FOB.

RUKI I – I don't...?

SUNNY Like fresh off the boat. Just move.

RUKI Oh, no! No, I was in Chanel in Tokyo, but they transfer me to the office here.

SUNNY Woah. That's – wow. Sorry, man.

RUKI Huh?

SUNNY No, it's just – no offence, but Clearday™ is like a big downgrade from Chanel. You like – fuck up? Get fired?

RUKI *(taken aback)* Oh! No!

SUNNY Oh. Shit. /Sorry.

RUKI No, no. I quit.

SUNNY ...Dude... why?

RUKI Uh. To be honest it was very cut-throat. There was a lot of – you know.

SUNNY Ah.

RUKI I want something, you know, less – less – you know.

SUNNY Well, we definitely are like that.

RUKI Yes?

SUNNY Oh yeah man, is super chill here. No corporate shit. We're like the Facebook of Asian cosmetics.

RUKI *(no idea what that means)* Okay.

(**PRIYA** *enters with her briefcase.*)

(*Much more in her element than we've seen her.*)

PRIYA Oh, great, Ruki.

RUKI Hi!

PRIYA How are you?

RUKI Good, yes. Excited.

PRIYA You're – you feel settled? You've had the tour?

RUKI Yes, yes, thank you. Sunny has been very... helpful.

SUNNY *(saluting)* Check.

PRIYA Great! Well, let me know if you need anything. We'll have a quick staff meeting when Built gets in.

RUKI Okay!

(*Exit* **PRIYA**.)

SUNNY Built is always late.

RUKI Built, I don't think I have met...

SUNNY She's Thailand.

RUKI Oh, okay, so there is Thailand and Japan and...?

SUNNY Wow, okay, so no one has briefed you.

RUKI No, I am sorry, not really. At the interview, Priya said you are expanding to Japan, but –

(The rest of the team filters in.)

BUILT Morning, ladies.

SUNNY It's midday, asshole.

BUILT You love me.

SUNNY Uh, I love you like I love –

PRIYA OKAY, everyone, let's give a warm welcome to our Office Manager, Ruki, who's also going to be heading up the new Japan division. Yay.

RUKI Hello. Hi.

PRIYA And I'd just like to say, Ruki – you're really joining a family here.

RUKI Thank you, yes.

PRIYA And – I mean, we discussed this a bit in your interview, but – the reason we're all here, the reason I founded Clearday™ in the first place, was to create an alternative to Asian corporate culture. Which is just – it's just so toxic.

RUKI Yes.

PRIYA And just because we've been so successful for a young brand –

SUNNY Like, unnaturally successful.

PRIYA – doesn't mean we've forgotten our roots. Which is all to say – let's keep that start-up mentality alive!

RUKI Yes! Okay!

PRIYA Great! So, let's dive right in. First off, the Double Black campaign is really taking off, thank you, Built.

BUILT Like, I'm a low-key genius, whatever.

PRIYA We're experiencing a sharp spike in repeat purchase, which, of course, is very good news. I'm not going to say the B-word –

SUNNY Bonus, baby.

PRIYA – but I think I can safely say that the board is fairly chuffed. So. Keep an eye out for that. Which, of course, brings us to the new range! Manufacturing?

SOO-JIN Yes, okay, the new samples are very good.

PRIYA Amazing.

SOO-JIN Four tones lighter in only two to three months.

PRIYA Ruki? You have a question?

RUKI Oh – I just...?

PRIYA Yes, yeah, shoot! We're very – you're probably getting this by now, we try to be very modern here. There's no presentations or anything, we just talk. We're a team. Totally democratic. Like a think tank.

RUKI Oh, okay, I wondered – how does it do that?

PRIYA What do you mean?

RUKI Only... is not true that most whitening creams are... fake?

PRIYA 'Placebos', Ruki, that's very good. Great work.

SUNNY You know what a drug cocktail is?

RUKI ...Yes?

SUNNY It's like that.

RUKI ...I – I don't –

SOO-JIN It is a very comprehensive combination treatment.

RUKI I – I'm sorry, I don't – so you're using many... bleaching agents?

PRIYA More like every bleaching agent.

SUNNY Just to the limit of the legal dosage.

BUILT Which, like, we adjust depending on where we sell it.

RUKI Oh. This... this is legal?

SOO-JIN It's...

PRIYA So now that you've signed the NDA, I can say that – while all our import-export is totally above water, totally legal, with our online sales it's...

RUKI I see.

PRIYA *(laughing)* As with most things to do with the internet, it's just a grey area.

RUKI Oh, okay, yes.

PRIYA Following so far?

RUKI Yes, I – yes.

PRIYA Try to use a clearer affirmation, if you can, Ruki, 'Yes, I understand.'

RUKI Okay. I understand. Thank you.

PRIYA Wonderful. *(to* **SOO-JIN***)* And where are we with the manufacturing lag?

SOO-JIN I will go to Shenzen next week, we are trying a new synthesizing method.

RUKI *(whispered, to* **SUNNY***)* What is Shenzen?

PRIYA *(laughing)* You don't have to – Shenzen is the site of our manufacturing and animal testing.

RUKI Wait, I'm sorry, you are organic?

PRIYA Yes.

RUKI But you do animal testing?

PRIYA Animal testing has nothing to do with being organic.

RUKI What animals do you test on?

PRIYA Black rats and rabbits, mostly.

RUKI *(a little deflated)* Oh.

SUNNY Ain't that bad. Actually it's kinda cute. They get these like little white blotches and shit.

PRIYA Moving right along to... development! Built? Do you want to –

BUILT All you, babe.

PRIYA Sure. *(rounding on the team)* So one of the conversations we've been having recently, you know, is about the direction of our brand, who we are as a brand. And of course, what distinguishes our product in local markets, right, is our facility with English, our high-quality branding. But so far – and feel free to chip in on this, Built – we just feel like we haven't really tapped into a *universal* message, one that transcends the local market. Because the question of why women want whitening cream, is, it's so culturally specific.

SUNNY South Asians got the whole caste thing.

PRIYA Exactly, yes.

SUNNY Thai women wanna look like Korean women.

PRIYA Yes, thank you –

SUNNY Korean women wanna look like dolls.

PRIYA Sunny. We talked about the talking.

SUNNY Ha. Sorry. Zip.

PRIYA Anyway, we've been trying to work out, you know, is there a unifying message for our brand, one that doesn't so much target separate national markets, but Asia in general. And so I think we need to reframe our... let's say our guiding question. Instead of asking why women *want* whitening cream, let's ask ourselves, why do women *need* whitening cream? Ruki.

RUKI Yes?

PRIYA Thoughts?

RUKI Oh. Uh. Why they need...

PRIYA Whitening cream.

RUKI But... they don't.

PRIYA Ah, but, Ruki. I'm not talking about what they literally need. I'm talking about what they *emotionally* need. Does that makes sense?

RUKI Ah, yes, okay.

PRIYA So? *(beat)* Women *need* whitening cream, women need beauty products in general, because women – *all* women – hate the way they look. They hate themselves. *(beat)* Which brings us to... White Pearl. Built, would you –

BUILT Yeah, so, like, Priya had this idea –

PRIYA It was a collaborative –

BUILT Sure, whatever. So like, instead of creating different products for different countries, we introduce like... a global whitening cream range.

PRIYA The White Pearl range.

BUILT But with each product in the range, we also, like, target things women hate about themselves, like, acne, pockmarks, cellulite, scars. So if you hate multiple things about your skin –

SUNNY Boom, son.

BUILT – you have to buy multiple creams.

PRIYA Ruki.

RUKI Yes?

PRIYA What do you think?

RUKI Me?

PRIYA Of course. We want your input.

RUKI Oh. Um. Okay.

PRIYA But if you don't have a –

RUKI No, okay – um, so... maybe there is another... aspect?

PRIYA Another aspect. Okay. And what's that?

RUKI Shame?

PRIYA Shame. That's interesting. Go on.

RUKI Okay, uh, because girls, obviously, they are hating the way they look, but, they are not wanting to... admit this?

PRIYA Interesting.

RUKI So basically – basically I am thinking that your way to sell to everybody is maybe – um, I'm thinking – okay, maybe that you are organic? You know, like Sk–II, marketed as a very clean healthy product. And actually minimizing the whitening aspect, like it is almost a side effect. We do not say 'Pearl makes your skin white', we say 'Pearl makes your skin...clear.' Or maybe...light – no, bright. Yes, okay, maybe both: Clear and Bright. So then maybe girls will... I mean they will still buy it because they want to be white, you know, but this way there is less, you know. Shame.

(A beat.)

SUNNY Dude. This girl a fucking genius.

PRIYA Clear and Bright. Bloody beautiful. Yes, Ruki. Yes. *(to* **XIAO***)* Xiao. Xiao?

XIAO Hm? Sorry.

PRIYA Everything okay?

XIAO Yes.

PRIYA Great! So. DBB. Television.

XIAO Oh.

PRIYA You said they had a treatment?

XIAO Oh, yes.

PRIYA So! Fill us in.

Scene Two: <u>4.2 Million</u>

(Back to the present.)

(The second bathroom stall.)

(**MARCEL** *plays with phone as he buttons his fly.*)

(**BUILT** *is also on her phone.*)

MARCEL I forgot how good you are. I have remember it was the best but I forget just *how* good, you know? Your mouth, is like... like a *vacuum. (beat)* And do not worry. I am an honourable man. The video, it will go down. Your little embezzling secret, this is safe with me. I will take care of you, baby. Like always. *(beat)* What are you doing?

BUILT I'm getting you an Uber.

MARCEL Okay, I meet you in the lobby.

(Beat.)

BUILT Say what now?

MARCEL You need to get your bag, yes?

BUILT ...

MARCEL I get the car to wait, it's no problem.

BUILT Are – wait – *what*?

MARCEL Why, you want to meet at the airport?

BUILT I – how – did you just like fall into a temporary coma and like miss everything that just happened?

MARCEL Ah?

BUILT That is not the fucking deal, Marcel. The deal is you vanish. Like now. Like *yesterday.*

MARCEL Ah, of course, the 'deal'.

BUILT No, not the 'deal', the deal, Marcel, the deal we literally just made.

MARCEL Built, baby. You can drop with the game now.

BUILT I'm not – there's no *game*, Marcel!

MARCEL Uh-huh, okay, sure. There is no 'game'.

BUILT Oh my God, I'm gonna be fucking sick, Marcel, I swear to fucking God, I swear to *fucking God*, there is no *game,* I am not playing, I like need you to *go*, I like need to go you *now*.

MARCEL Wait, but –

BUILT Nnn, no, this is not happening, la la la, this is not happening, you are going to *leave*, you are gonna get in the Uber that is downstairs and then you are gonna be gone from my life.

MARCEL But –

BUILT Your driver's name is Lee.

MARCEL Baby –

BUILT It's a Red Toyota.

MARCEL Hey! Stop! Okay! What /are you doing?

BUILT DID I FUCKING STUTTER, MARCEL! GET THE FUCK OUT OF HERE!

(Beat.)

MARCEL But... but... you sucked my...

BUILT Oh my God.

MARCEL I mean, you have just – you have just knelt here... I have just come in your *mouth*, and this... this was nothing to you?

BUILT And now he's being redirected.

MARCEL You do this to make me *leave*?

BUILT He's being –

MARCEL What is *wrong* with you?

BUILT Your driver. Is being.

MARCEL I mean, I know you are fucked up –

BUILT Redirected.

MARCEL But this is – this is crazy even for you.

BUILT Aaand he's gone. *(beat)* Okay, well. Enjoy the, like, stall. I have to get back to the like crisis situation you created, so. You can get your own fucking car.

(She turns to go.)

MARCEL Wait, don't, I –

BUILT I am so done talking to you, Marcel, it's not even –

MARCEL I can't get the Uber.

BUILT Excuse me?

MARCEL I don't have this, Uber. I don't have it.

BUILT Um, so I feel like there's like an analogue solution to this problem? Oh, that's right, you walk downstairs and flag yourself a *fucking cab.*

MARCEL I don't...

BUILT Also I *know* you have data roaming, you've been feminazi-ing all over YouTube today, so. What's the problem?

MARCEL The flight here, to Singapore, it was... it was... I use all I have. Okay? I use it.

BUILT I have literally zero idea what you're saying.

MARCEL *Nom de Dieu*, you want me to say out loud? Okay, fine, I am out of money, I do not have any money.

(BUILT stares at him blankly for a moment.)

BUILT *(starting to laugh)* Oh. Oh, this is, this is too good.

MARCEL Okay, just –

BUILT You're *broke*?

MARCEL I am between job.

BUILT What about 'the cover of the Japanese Vogue'? What about 'big success'?

MARCEL See, this – this is your problem, Built, you cannot see anything that is not money.

BUILT Wait, so you're telling me, you spent –

MARCEL Success is different for an artist.

BUILT – on a flight to *Singapore* –

MARCEL You see now how much I /love you.

BUILT – for this batshit fucking crazy *scheme* –

MARCEL I will *ruin* myself –

BUILT – and you thought – you actually for real thought that I was gonna get back together with you? And then what? Marcel? What was your plan? Oh! Oh I know! Was it that I was gonna pay for all your shit? That you would get me back, and then I would pay for all your fucking *shit*, like I used to?

MARCEL No!

BUILT No?

(Beat.)

MARCEL Okay, something like that, yes.

BUILT Oh my God. Here I am thinking I'm, oh my God – and you're – you're whoring yourself out.

MARCEL No, it's not –

BUILT You're literally whoring yourself out!

MARCEL This is not about the money!

BUILT EVERYTHING IS ABOUT THE MONEY, MARCEL! MONEY IS EVERYTHING AND EVERYTHING IS

MONEY! AND YOU'RE EITHER TOO FUCKING STUPID
OR TOO FUCKING CRAZY TO SEE THAT!

(Beat.)

MARCEL Okay, so, you clearly have some mental issue going on
here, so, I am just going to go. Okay? I am going.

BUILT I'll give you a thousand dollars to admit you're a whore.

MARCEL What?

BUILT Better yet, a dirty whore. Yeah, say 'I'm a dirty whore',
Marcel, and I'll give you a thousand Singaporean dollars.
Cash. You take cash, right?

MARCEL I don't –

BUILT Oh, you don't want a thousand Singaporean dollars?
Because that's like eight hundred euros.

MARCEL I am an honorable man.

BUILT Two thousand.

MARCEL You can't just –

BUILT Three thousand.

MARCEL I don't –

BUILT *(she produces it from her bag)* Five thousand. Right here.
You wanna count it? Five words, five thousand dollars. Seems
fair, right? A K a word?

MARCEL I –

BUILT Yes?

MARCEL I – okay, fine, I... I am a...

BUILT Mm?

MARCEL I am...

BUILT A...?

MARCEL I am a... *(muttered)* Iamdirtywhore.

(**MARCEL** *goes to grab the wad of cash. She holds it back.*)

BUILT Mm. Not quite.

MARCEL *Salope de merde.* Go to the fucking hell.

BUILT Mm, but then *you'd* be there, so...

MARCEL I AM A DIRTY WHORE, OKAY? YOU WIN! I AM A DIRTY WHORE! YOU WIN! YOU ALWAYS WIN! I AM A DIRTY WHORE. I AM A DIRTY WHORE!

(*She throws the wad of cash at him.*)

(*He gathers the notes off the floor. He stands.*)

BUILT Good girl.

(*He spits in her face.*)

(*He exits.*)

(*She wipes her face.*)

(*She throws up in the toilet.*)

Scene Three: <u>4.8 million</u>

(The conference room.)

*(***PRIYA*** *is scouring the news.)*

*(***SUNNY*** *nurses her drink.)*

PRIYA Are you reading this?

SUNNY You know I major in journalism?

PRIYA 30% loss of subscriptions. Sixty-thousand orders returned.

SUNNY Shoulda been a journalist.

PRIYA Withdrawals from Paragon and Junction 8.

SUNNY I woulda been tsai* journalist.

PRIYA *(another tab)* Oh, look, apparently we've 'shocked the global community'. What does that even mean, the global community? Since when was that a *thing*? Global *communitas*.

SUNNY Let it go lah.

PRIYA And here's the bleeding *Bangkok Post* with their two cents: 'A disgusting illustration of the deep-seated racism that permeates the Asian media climate.'

SUNNY Eh, that's just uppity Thai fuckers.

PRIYA No. No. Don't undersell this. I found damning articles in Hindi too.

SUNNY Dude, you speak Hindi?

PRIYA Well, no, not really, but I got the fucking gist.

SUNNY Yo, didn't you live in Mumbai 'til you were like eleven?

PRIYA *(withering stare)* And?

---

* Hokkien: to be really good at something.

SUNNY Yeah, no, no worry.

PRIYA Oh, what, because I don't speak Hindi –

SUNNY Woah! Bro!

PRIYA I'm somehow 'alienated' –

SUNNY Bro! Chill the eff out! I ain't the one accusing you of being an 'inauthentic' Asian and shit. Chh.

(**SOO-JIN** *gingerly opens the cracked door. A momentary stand-off.* **PRIYA** *and* **SUNNY** *ignore her.*)

(*At length:*)

SOO-JIN I... I have something to say to you.

PRIYA That's hilarious, because I have nothing to say to you.

SOO-JIN It is important.

PRIYA Oh, oh, it's important, is it?

SOO-JIN Yes.

PRIYA So, hm, I'm sorry – after you've undermined Sunny's press release, embarked on a racist tirade –

SUNNY – break company /property –

PRIYA – yes, thank you, Sunny – broke the *fucking door* – now is the time you pick to tell us something important.

SOO-JIN It is *very* important.

PRIYA Oh, well, if it's *very* important, then by all means.

SOO-JIN May I sit?

PRIYA No.

SOO-JIN ...I – I may not sit?

PRIYA No. You may not sit. You may deliver your *very important* news from the door.

SOO-JIN Why – why may I not sit?

PRIYA Might break the fuckin' table, innit?

(**SUNNY** *snorts into her whisky.*)

SOO-JIN It is about dosage.

PRIYA Yeah? What about it?

SOO-JIN Before, when you were – when you were angry with me, and you were saying that I should not speak unless – unless I am speaking of my area of expertise, which is the chemistry. This made me think, now that we are under media scrutiny, I think maybe it is not good for me to... I think it is time you should know some things.

PRIYA ...Things.

SOO-JIN I think I should – in case there is scrutiny, I should... it is maybe time I should tell some things.

PRIYA (*suddenly very measured*) Soo. Sit down.

(**SOO-JIN** *sits.* **PRIYA** *is very still.*)

SUNNY Uh. No follow.

PRIYA Sunny. (*motions for her to shut up*) Soo – talk.

SOO-JIN Okay. You remember the Double Black campaign?

PRIYA Double Black...?

SOO-JIN This is maybe one year ago, online for South Asia? We spread this myth in secret online campaign, you know, use White Pearls twice a day, get twice as white. Stop using White Pearls, get /twice as black.

PRIYA Twice as black. Sure, that one. What does this /have to –

SOO-JIN So we have a big rise in sales, really huge surprise rise –

PRIYA Don't set the bloody scene. I was here.

SOO-JIN Okay – you remember I take a trip to Shenzen? To see if we can make manufacture – to reduce lag time?

PRIYA Yeah, okay, you found a new way of synthesizing, or I don't know, using soap fat or whatever.

SOO-JIN I... lied.

PRIYA ...

SUNNY ...

PRIYA You...?

SOO-JIN The main reason for lag time, the main slowing down – I don't know what you remember, but this was costing us a lot of money, a lot of sales, and we were just growing as a business, so it was very important to be more efficient –

PRIYA What do you mean you *lied*?

SOO-JIN The lag was not in synthesizing. It was just that we are doing so many variations with the dosage. We are constantly changing the quantity of bleaching agents for different countries, and it was wasting time. It was wasting time and money. So I recommended –

PRIYA Don't tell me what I think you're about to tell me.

SOO-JIN I recommended, at the time –

PRIYA Oh my God, /oh my God.

SOO-JIN – that we – instead of –

PRIYA Don't finish that sentence.

SOO-JIN ...

PRIYA How /long –

SUNNY Wah lau eh*.

SOO-JIN Yes.

PRIYA How long – I can't breathe – how long have we been exporting – oh God – how long have we exceeded the legal dosage?

---

* Singlish (Hokkien/Teochew): exclamation of shock.

(Beat.)

SOO-JIN ...For which country?

(Beat.)

SUNNY MOTHER/FUCKER.

PRIYA WHICH – OH MY GOD. WHICH *COUNTRY*?

SOO-JIN We were small enough company at the time, I did not think – there was no way anyone would ever test the chemical constitution for the cream, I did not think anyone would /notice.

PRIYA WHICH – you realize this is – you realize we've broken *dozens* of consumer safety laws.

SOO-JIN Yes.

PRIYA *Dozens* of *laws. Laws.* In *multiple countries.* Countries which have *OPEN-AIR PRISONS.*

SUNNY *(downing her whisky)* We proper kana sai,* bro.

PRIYA Who knows about this?

SOO-JIN Us three. And... and Xiao.

PRIYA Xiao? How the bloody – how does *Xiao* know?

SOO-JIN She is... *(realizing this for the first time)* my friend.

SUNNY Lucky her.

PRIYA I'm going to forget you just said that. Who else? People on the ground?

SOO-JIN On the...?

PRIYA In Shenzen.

SOO-JIN Oh – uh. Yes.

PRIYA Yes? Who?

---

* Singlish (Malay/Hokkien): 'in deep shit'.

SOO-JIN The – uh – the factory owner. But he – he is a very simple man, he does not understand anything about the chemicals. He knows we make adjustments, but he thinks this is all legal.

PRIYA What about bribes? Who did you bribe? Local bureaucrats? Party officials?

SOO-JIN No! No – I – it is only us four who know, okay? That is all.

PRIYA So what you're telling me – you're telling me that you have pulled off this very elaborate, this highly illegal – you're saying that our brand, one of the *most widely used cosmetic brands in Asia*, has been selling whitening cream legally considered to be toxic in *multiple countries* – for over a year – and only four people know about it.

SOO-JIN Yes.

PRIYA And three of them are in this room.

SOO-JIN Yes.

PRIYA So. So. So what I really need to know from you now –

SOO-JIN It is very unlikely.

PRIYA ...?

SOO-JIN It is very unlikely anyone will find out.

PRIYA It is?

SOO-JIN I would say almost impossible. You need a lab test for very specific chemical agents. And no one is looking for specific agents, and so no one will do this.

PRIYA So –

SOO-JIN Almost impossible.

SUNNY Then WHY IN JESUS NAME YOU TELL US, BRO?

SOO-JIN We are in trouble now with this video, so on the small chance – I think it is important, in case something goes wrong. That you are knowing the full story.

PRIYA The full story.

SOO-JIN Yes.

PRIYA The full fucking story.

SOO-JIN Yes?

PRIYA See, this – this is what I really hate about you homeland Asian cunts. You love to get on your high horse about how uppity we are, how superior we are. How I'm a bitch because I think I'm better than you, like I unfairly lord over you and I unfairly get better jobs because boohoo I have an undergrad from UCL and speak English with some degree of fucking *finesse*. But you know what? I *am* better than you. I *am* smarter than you. And the reason I'm smarter than you, is that unlike you, my Western education has equipped me with a skill known as *lateral thinking*. You know what *lateral thinking* is, Soo-Jin?

SOO-JIN I /don't think –

PRIYA No. Of course you bloody don't. Because they don't teach lateral thinking in the totalitarian shithole /from whence you spring.

SOO-JIN I am not from North Korea.

PRIYA Well, let me tell you, Soo-Jong-il, lateral thinking is a *highly* useful skill to have. *Highly* useful. It allows you to see other *pathways*. Find creative *solutions*. Not just confine your mind to the fascist schools of thought that have been provided for it. For instance – see, in your mind, you with your bullshit Korean education where you sung the national anthem seventeen times a day and got hit with a cane whenever you got your timetables wrong – see, in your mind, it makes perfect sense to report your own illegal activity to your superiors. Blab in case of trouble. Up the chain of command, yeah? Confess your sins, the Party forgives?

SOO-JIN You –

PRIYA LET ME FINISH. So you come here, all repentant like, confessing that you've done this crazy illegal thing, searching for some kind of absolution. But see, if *I* had been in your shoes, if *I* had done a crazy illegal thing, *I* with my *lateral thinking skills* could have thought a step further, and deduced that my superiors – *who are not in any way responsible for my mistakes* – would not want to know that shit. I would deduce with my *lateral thinking skills* that they would not want to be privy to this information because it makes them *accessories* to criminal activity. Are you following me so far?

SOO-JIN I am following you perfectly.

PRIYA See, honestly, Soo, that surprises me.

SOO-JIN I following you better than you think.

PRIYA ...

SUNNY ...

PRIYA What is that supposed to mean?

SOO-JIN You underestimating me. You are always underestimating me. I have a Masters Degree in Biochemistry, you think I am not able of doing *lateral thinking*?

PRIYA Well, thus /far –

SOO-JIN *I want you to be accessories.*

PRIYA ...

SUNNY ...

SOO-JIN ...

PRIYA ...

SUNNY So, there's been like too many twists and reveals today, I am mega confuse.

SOO-JIN Sunny – shut the fuck up.

SUNNY Woooaah brah.

SOO-JIN I am telling /you what happens now.

SUNNY The fuck is happening?

SOO-JIN You will be going to the board tomorrow. You are saying it is DBB's fault only, and no one should be being fired. In the next year, you are campaigning for a salary raise for Xiao because of the unstable situation in China.

SUNNY Uh.

SOO-JIN This is also you accepting my three months' notice. In the next months, I am finding my own excellent replacement, who will also be South Korean. You are giving me enormous severance and amazing recommendation letters. You are giving me a bigger living allowance in Singapore to help with the difficult transition back to South Korea.

SUNNY Are you *HIGH?*

SOO-JIN From now on, you are treating Xiao and Ruki with respect. You are treating them as equals on this team. You are not using them like they are your Asian housemaids. You are giving them decency and respect, as they deserve. You are doing all of this, or I am talking to the press. And before you are saying 'If you do this, you will be the person getting in trouble' – I will contact the newspaper anonymously. I will already be in Korea where they will not extradite. I will already have buried my paper trail. So this chemical shitstorm will only be leading back to you. So. You must do this. Or you are all *fucked.*

(A long beat.)

*(**SUNNY**'s jaw could hit the floor.)*

*(**PRIYA** collapses in a riotous fit of laughter. Hyena-worthy.)*

PRIYA *(cackling)* Who – who put you up to this?

SOO-JIN No one.

PRIYA It was – it was Xiao, wasn't it? It was, wasn't it? My word, that sneaky Ching Chong cunt!

SOO-JIN No one has made me do this.

PRIYA What *is it* with you two – ha – I mean, are you – are you *fucking* or something? You're fucking, aren't you?

SOO-JIN I am not –

PRIYA Scissor – scissoring in the office loo!

SOO-JIN I am not – I am doing this for me. For me only.

PRIYA I can't – hoo! Okay, okay. Hoo! Okay. Let's say, for a minute, just for my own amusement, I entertain this sort of poorly thought-out attempt at 'blackmail', over this claim of – yeah sure, 'illegal activity'. Which, by the by, I'm increasingly doubting ever actually happened. But just because today has already been such a bloody *fun time*, let me entertain your hypothetical *demands* for a moment. Who would you like to trade up instead?

SOO-JIN Trade...

PRIYA Aren't you the *scientist*? This is the law of bloody entropy, darling. This is the immutable truth of the universe. Something has to be destroyed for something to be created. And somebody is getting *destroyed* today.

SOO-JIN I don't –

PRIYA Come on, sweetheart. Use your newfound lateral thinking skills. There has been a PR disaster, and somebody is getting fired for it. That is a known quantity. So if that isn't going to be Xiao, I'd like you to tell me which one of you *bimbos* it should be.

SOO-JIN ...

PRIYA Or did you not get that far in your little blackmail plot?

(**BUILT** *rockets in, clutching her phone.*)

(*She is shaking.*)

BUILT Do you have it open?

SUNNY Bro, this is like the literal worst /time –

BUILT Do you. Have it. Open.

SUNNY You mean the /video?

BUILT Yes, is it open, do /you have it open?

SUNNY *(referring to* **PRIYA***'s laptop)* Yeah bro, why?

BUILT Close it.

SUNNY What the fuck? /Why?

BUILT Close it now. Close it right /fucking now.

PRIYA Built, what's –

　　*(***BUILT*** slams* **PRIYA***'s laptop shut.)*

SUNNY *(looking at her phone)* Wait, Irigaray post a new video?

BUILT DON'T –

SUNNY Woaaah, is that a blowj –

　　*(***BUILT*** bounds across the room, grabs* **SUNNY***'s phone
　　and – in the same motion – hurls it.)*

　　(It collides squarely with the door.)

　　(The door shatters spectacularly. Everyone screams.)

Scene Four: <u>5 million</u>

(The bathroom stall.)

(XIAO still curled up on the floor.)

(RUKI enters gingerly, with a cup of tea.)

RUKI Are you okay?

XIAO ...

RUKI Can I sit?

XIAO ...

> *(RUKI sits).*

RUKI I brought some tea.

XIAO ...

RUKI I will – okay, I will put it on the floor here.

> *(RUKI places the mug on the floor.)*

XIAO ...Thank you.

RUKI It's – you're welcome.

XIAO ...

RUKI Um. Xiao, you have been here now for – it's just, are you – is it you are still in here – you are worried about being fired? Or something else?

XIAO *(very quietly)* Soo will fix.

RUKI ...Sorry, Soo...?

XIAO No. I am not worry.

RUKI Oh – okay.

> *(Beat.)*

XIAO Thank you. For the tea.

RUKI Oh! You're welcome.

XIAO It is green tea?

RUKI Yes! I thought – but if you do not /like –

XIAO No, green tea is – I like green tea.

*(Beat. **XIAO** picks up the tea.)*

(She doesn't drink it.)

(Another beat.)

RUKI Uh, Xiao, um.

XIAO Yes?

RUKI You know they are having me check for news at the moment, for Japanese articles about the video.

XIAO Okay?

RUKI And I read something – you know this big anti-corruption case that is happening in China? With this man, the second in command in the Politburo?

XIAO ...

RUKI And I notice – I noticed that his last name is Chen... and your last name is also Chen... Maybe it is a common name, but... you know, you have been so upset these last months... I wondered maybe, I wanted to check... are you related to this man?

XIAO ...

RUKI Xiao?

XIAO ...

RUKI You are?

XIAO No.

RUKI Oh. Oh. Okay. But – you know I am googling him and it says he has a daughter who is called Xiao.

XIAO ...

RUKI But maybe it is a common name.

XIAO It is very common name.

RUKI Okay. But I thought maybe –

XIAO I –

RUKI But you don't have/ to –

XIAO I –

(**XIAO** *starts to cry again.*)

RUKI Oh, Xiao. Why did you not tell anyone?

XIAO I tell Soo.

RUKI Why not Priya? Why not me? Maybe we could help.

XIAO Because...because you not liking me!

RUKI W-what?

XIAO You not like me.

RUKI Xiao, you think I don't like you?

XIAO Of course.

RUKI Why do you think I don't like you?

XIAO Because.

RUKI Because why?

XIAO Because.

RUKI No, why?

XIAO Because...you are Japanese.

(*Beat.*)

RUKI You – you think I – you think because I am Japanese
and you are Chinese, and because we are not supposed
to like each other – you think because of this I don't like
you?

XIAO Yes.

RUKI No!

XIAO No?

RUKI No! I like you!

XIAO Oh.

RUKI Of course I like you.

XIAO Oh – well – I – I like you too.

RUKI Oh. Thank you.

XIAO You're welcome.

RUKI Well. Okay.

(They sit in silence for a few moments.)

XIAO Ruki?

RUKI Yes?

XIAO You use *White Pearl*? Ever?

RUKI Oh, um. No. Never. You?

XIAO Yes. Before I start work here.

RUKI I see.

XIAO But my first day, Soo is telling me to stop. She tell me all the danger. She is always like big sister to me. She is such a good person. Not like us. She not obsessed with beauty and cosmetic like us. She see through it. I think because she is scientist. After this job, I think maybe she is doing something really good. Like cure cancer. Not like me. I do not know how to do another job.

RUKI I'm sure you do.

XIAO No. I really do not.

(Beat.)

RUKI I – I did.

XIAO Mmm?

RUKI I used *Pearl*.

XIAO Oh.

RUKI My first three months.

XIAO At Clearday™?

RUKI Yes.

XIAO After you are already starting work here?

RUKI We got a big discount. I thought, you know, I would just try it. To see.

XIAO But – even when you are knowing all the danger?

RUKI I thought, you know, they say it makes such a difference in only three months. How much damage can it do in three months? Cannot be any worse than smoking or using a microwave.

XIAO Oh. Maybe.

RUKI And everyone in the office was so – it was stupid.

XIAO Well, at least you stop now.

RUKI Yes.

XIAO Did it work? You get more white?

RUKI No.

XIAO Oh.

RUKI But I – I think I – I was maybe already too white.

XIAO Oh. Can you be too white?

(**RUKI** *doesn't know.*)

(*They sit in silence.*)

(**XIAO** *drinks her tea.*)

Scene Five: <u>5.3 million</u>

THARUN KUMAR The makers of this advertisement deserve to be put behind bars.

KEMIT TRILL If this was a US brand they would finished.

<u>5.6 million</u>

MASSIVE ATTACK Anyone else not really offended but find this extremely hilarious?

HAVEN2MAC YT I'm black and it's funny.

VINEET PANDE I'm brown as fuck, and i laughed hysterically. Why westerners make such a big deal about race??

RESURGAM75 you are wrong. I'm a black guy from the UK. I don't think I've ever seen an advert that was more insulting or ignorant.

<u>6.1 million</u>

BLUECORE My friend told me that when she was 14 she saw ad like this on tv she sat in the bath for hours trying to wash her dark skin away. I felt like a bad person for laughing at them.

DEUCES MOFO your friend is fucking retarded if she made it to 14 and thought she could wash her skin color off.

<u>6.6 million</u>

This in increasingly rapid succession:

CARTAGENA MENDOZA We just need another pearl harbor attack is all

AVERAGE USER Pearl Harbor was by Japanese not Chinese you stupid fuck.

PREACHER GERALD WHITE Everyone knows that blacks are inferior.

SANDY SANDY gross, who wants Yellow skin and slant eyes.

WINTERCHILD Does it work with Arabs and Turks too?

BAD GAMER Slaves stay slaves

DUKEDVL69 Shut the fuck up you ignorant shit.

ARISINGHERO jews are racist too

LUDWIG ADELMEIER black people produce the most body odor

NEON THE WOLF GO DIE IN A FUCK'IN HOLE

LEBRUH CHINGCHONG100

JOJO GUNNE get over it moaning snowflakes

SANDY SANDY D-M Dirty Ape

PAULUS DE KENEZY Liberals has no sense of humor.

(Beat.)

ONISCIA BRUNO This comment section is toxic.

Scene Six: <u>The Video You Requested Is No Longer Available</u>

(The conference room.)

*(**RUKI** carefully steps around the glass, sweeping.)*

(The rest of the team sits around the table.)

(The whisky is gone.)

BUILT I'm fired, aren't I?

PRIYA /Ab-so-lute-ly.

SUNNY Gurl *helll* yes.

    (Beat).

XIAO Am... am I fired? /Because I –

SOO-JIN Priya, she didn't /know –

PRIYA No.

SUNNY Eh?

SOO-JIN /She's not?

XIAO /I'm not?

PRIYA She's not.

XIAO /Oh.

SUNNY Dude, what?

PRIYA Well. Built's out. *(to **SOO-JIN**)* Decidedly firing your ass.

SUNNY Hold up, because of the –

PRIYA Yes.

SUNNY But what if she –

PRIYA Sunny.

SUNNY But isn't she –

PRIYA Sunny, for fuck's – try to keep up? She made it up. *(auddenly unsure, to* **SOO**.*)* You...made it up. You made it up.

(*Beat.* **SOO-JIN** *looks away.*)

(**SUNNY** *claps.*)

SUNNY Yo, for a second I genuinely thought we like poisoned hella people!

BUILT I mean, like, technically, we / have.

PRIYA I'm sorry, do you work here? No. So. Built's out. Soo's out. And I'd say we need at least two-thirds of the office to stay afloat, so, for the present moment, Xiao stays. For the *present moment*. Or does that not sit well with everyone?

(*Stunned beat.*)

XIAO Priya, I, you don't know – thank /you –

PRIYA Don't make me change my mind.

XIAO No. No, from now I will not –

SUNNY Dude, she means shut the eff up.

XIAO Oh. Yes.

(*Beat.*)

SUNNY *(to* **BUILT***)* So he's like... your ex?

BUILT Yep.

SUNNY Bro. You got shitty taste lah.

BUILT Sunny. Eat shit and die.

SUNNY Yo, harsh.

BUILT Oh my God! Who do you think you're fooling with your fucking 'yo' and 'dude' and 'bro', like everyone knows you've never left Singapore, you fucking try-hard bitch.

(*Beat.*)

SUNNY Ohhh, girl, you done it now. *(to* **PRIYA***)* So before they took down the – you know, the /blowj – the video?

PRIYA Wow, I *really* don't want to hear any more about that.

SUNNY No – the vid –

PRIYA 'White Pearl Necklace.' Tasteful.

SUNNY – had the description 'Built Suttikul is an embezzling whore.'

(**BUILT** *cringes*).

PRIYA Oh. Hm.

SUNNY Felt you'd wanna know that.

PRIYA Hm.

SUNNY *(to* **BUILT***)* So. You wanna –

BUILT I like really /don't.

PRIYA Oh, wait. Is that the exchange rate thing?

BUILT ...You know about that?

PRIYA Oh yeah, that's nothing. I do that with rupees. That's fine. This is Asia. Everyone gets a cut. It's just how you do business.

(**XIAO** *starts hysterically crying.*)

SUNNY Woah.

PRIYA *(laughing again)* For fuck's – what is it now?

RUKI She is sensitive because her /fa –

XIAO No. No. It – it is nothing, I am just so – I am so happy. To still – still have job.

SOO-JIN No, that's –

XIAO *(still crying)* Soo, no – don't – thank you. I am – h-happy. I am so h-happy. Thank you – th–thank you.

SUNNY Yeesh, girl, the job ain't *that* good.

PRIYA *(still laughing)* You're welcome. Just – enough with the crying, yeah? Enough.

XIAO *(still crying)* I am s-sorry –

PRIYA *(still laughing)* No. I didn't say apologize. I said stop crying.

XIAO *(still crying)* I – I am –

PRIYA *(still laughing)* Xiao. Hoo. Xiao, listen to me. From now on, no crying, okay? There will be no crying in this office. It makes your face look like a – a placenta, ha, and it gives me a fucking migraine. So if you – hoo, wow, I actually can't stop – if you want to keep working here, for the love of all things holy, stop crying. Xiao, stop crying. Stop crying. Stop crying. Stop crying. Xiao, you keep crying and I'll fire you.

XIAO *(still crying)* I am trying!

PRIYA *(rage into blind rage)* Stop crying. Stop crying.

XIAO *(still crying)* I am trying!

PRIYA Xiao? Xiao. Stop. Xiao? Ohh, Xiao. Keep crying, you ugly bitch, keep crying, I fucking dare you. I will fire you so hard. Xiao. Stop. Stop. STOP CRYING!

*(A horrifying moment where everyone waits to see if **XIAO** can stop crying. I don't know if you've ever witnessed someone hysterically crying and trying to force themselves to stop – it's awful.)*

(But she does it.)

(Beat.)

Christ.

(Beat.)

XIAO *(muttered)* 洋狗 (yáng gǒu).

*(**SUNNY** snorts.)*

PRIYA What did you call me? *(to* **SUNNY***)* What did she call me?

SUNNY Uh, yeah, dunno.

PRIYA The fuck you don't, what did she call me? *(beat)* What did she call me?

SUNNY Nothing. Nothing, just, like *(struggling to contain her laughter)* ...like a... like a 红毛 (âng-môh) lah.

(**XIAO** *cracks up.*)

PRIYA What? What's that?

SUNNY *(really laughing)* You know, like 鬼婆 (gwáipo).

XIAO Or, or, 洋鬼子 (yángguǐzi)!

PRIYA Hey. Stop that.

RUKI *(getting it, laughing)* Oh, ohhh, you mean 外人 (gaijin)!

PRIYA What?

SOO-JIN *(laughing)* Oh, 코쟁이 (ko jaeng ee)!

RUKI Oh, 코쟁이 (ko jaeng ee)?

SOO-JIN Yes.

RUKI That's similar, for us, 外人 (gaijin).

SOO-JIN *(sounding it out)* 外人 (gaijin).

RUKI Yes, yes!

PRIYA How are you – what the fuck are you saying?

BUILT *(getting the joke)* Oh! Oh! ฝรั่ง (farang)!

RUKI *(sounding it out)* ฝรั่ง (farang).

BUILT ฝรั่ง (farang).

RUKI ฝรั่ง (farang).

BUILT Yes, yes, or really for her, you know, แขก (khaek).

XIAO Oh, oh, we have that too, 阿三 (ā sān).

PRIYA Hey! Cut it out!

(*Everyone except* **PRIYA** *in hysterics.*)

BUILT (*pointing at* **PRIYA**) ไอ้ฝรั่งดอง (ai farang dong)!

XIAO (*laughing hysterically, pointing at* **PRIYA**) 咖喱人 (gālírén) (*at* **SUNNY**) 香蕉 (xiāngjiāo)!

SOO-JIN (*to* **XIAO**) 짱깨 (jjang gae)!

XIAO (*clutching* **RUKI**'s *arm, shaking with laughter*) 日本狗 (rìběn gǒu)!

RUKI (*laughing*) Oh, gou? Like a – (*She mimes a dog.*)

XIAO Yes!

RUKI Oh, that is so bad!

XIAO I know!

(*The women are in fits of laughter, hurling racial slurs at each other. Aching, side-splitting, weeping.* **PRIYA** *doesn't understand. She looks around at the women clutching each other, laughing uproariously.*)

PRIYA Why is that funny? What are you – I don't – why is that funny? (*beat*) Why is that funny?

End of Play

ABOUT THE AUTHOR

Anchuli Felicia King is a playwright, screenwriter and multidisciplinary artist of Thai-Australian descent.

As a playwright, King is interested in linguistic hybrids, digital cultures and globalization. Her plays have been produced by the Royal Court Theatre (London), Studio Theatre (Washington D.C.), American Shakespeare Center (Staunton), Melbourne Theatre Company (Melbourne), Sydney Theatre Company, National Theatre of Parramatta, and Belvoir Theatre (Sydney). Her play *Golden Shield* made its Off-Broadway debut at Manhattan Theatre Club in 2022.

King was a screenwriter on *The Baby*, a dark horror comedy produced by Sister Pictures for HBO/Sky, *The Twelve*, a trial drama for the Foxtel Group and *Deadloch*, a noir comedy and Amazon original series. She is writing on TV projects for HBO, A24, AMC, Sister Pictures, BBC Studios, Warner Bros, Amazon, Netflix, Easy Tiger, Lucky Chap Entertainment, Hoodlum Entertainment and the Australian Broadcasting Corporation.